RALPHY RACCOON

A Business Tale

TED HSU

ISBN: 978-1-4834-4199-3 (sc)
ISBN: 978-1-4834-4198-6 (e)

Library of Congress Control Number: 2015919151

Lulu Publishing Services rev. date: 12/21/2015

Dedication

To Sweet Bear, Cubs, Birdy and Bean

Introduction

Ralphy Raccoon is an amalgam of the hundreds of small business heroes with whom I have had the honor to have worked for, competed against, and struggled with.

Note to readers:

This is not entirely a children's book.

Nevertheless, it can be shared with children, with your guidance.

Be prepared for many questions about topics that aren't commonly discussed.

If you are serious about preparing for life's challenges, these topics are wonderful to ponder and discuss for adults and children alike.

Thank you Rebecca Cook and Nina Cattan for making this book a reality. Without your help, this book would still be ruminations in my mind.

Ralphy raccoon leaves school with dreams of the easy life.
Sally Squirrel smiles at Ralphy despite seeing much future strife.

The next day.

Ralphy asks a family friend, Wise Raccoon a question; "What is your secret to making lots of money?"

Wise Raccoon says, "Oh Ralphy there's no secret. You have to work hard, always give your best, and understand that it is not always going to be sunny."

Ralphy is upset that getting rich does not sound easy.
The hint of hard work makes him queasy.

Getting no help from family and no help from his friend,
Ralphy starts his business as the means to an end.

Ralphy thinks Wise Raccoon is hiding the real secret to wealth.
"I know he is rich, he has a bunch of workers. That must be his secret plan!
Then I too will hire a whole lot of workers as fast as I can!"

Ralphy quickly puts an ad online, and quickly they all come.
Only after he hires them he finds each animal is either lazy or dumb.

Ralphy had hired without much thought or care, he called it compassion.
The truth is he hired animals just like himself… all talk and no action!

Ralphy is shocked and outraged.
He is surprised by these animals, who do not work but still expect to get paid!

Ralphy looks the other way. The thought of rehiring makes him tired.
With all the work that's not happening the customers make sure it is Ralphy who gets fired!

Ralphy hires Marco Mole to manage all his animal troubles.
He is impressed with Mole's promise to get business to double.

Marco tells Ralphy his success secret with a slight frown.
"If you want to move up in life, you need to bring others down."

Ralphy knows that advice is wrong, but it seems to work so well.
I'm going to wait and see, I don't think others can really tell.

After Ralphy leaves, Marco destroys all of Ralphy's equipment on the job.
Marco shows Customer Owl the "worn out" tools and says Ralphy Raccoon is cheap and a slob.

"Give Ralphy's contract to me," says Marco Mole, "I will charge less, and you won't be neglected."
The Owl agrees, and poor Ralphy gets ejected.

Ralphy and what's left of his equipment lay in the parking lot after his company is fired.

Wise Raccoon drives by and asks, "Why do you look so disgusted?"
Ralphy says, "Neither my workers nor my customers can be trusted."

Wise Raccoon pauses and says,

"Everyone you associate with is in conflict because your values are cheap.
You all seek short cuts. If you folks can't think long-term, this is the company you must keep."

Hiring good employees is not easy, Ralphy now knew.
Once he set standards and hired only employees who cared, the business grew!

Ralphy enjoys success because he set standards for himself and others around him. However, Ralphy's personal spending becomes the concern.

He buys everything he sees, just on a whim.

Ralphy is spending lots of money on himself without regrets.
He soon learns that one cannot go spending money without first paying their debts.

Ralphy does not see a great trouble coming. His over spending has caused his debts to mount.
Angry, unpaid animals show him that a business is a business and not a private bank account.

The unpaid workers go running to the Man without fail.
And quickly, agents from the Raccoon Republic show up for little Ralphy's tail!

The Republic always thinks small businesses are full of experiments that go sour.
They will make an example with the little troublemaker and make him feel their power.

The Raccoon Republic is a free country, or so they say.
Ralphy soon learns that only the Republic can print money and call it pay.

With all of his belongings seized,
Ralphy Raccoon is back on his knees.

"Oh, Wise Raccoon, getting ahead is so hard!" sobs Ralphy.

Wise Raccoon says to Ralphy:
"To succeed you must be thrifty, even when your revenues grow.
Show respect for every nickel, only then your bottom line will show."

In Ralphy's darkest hour, an old friend, the Wordy Birdy, flutters in.

"I have been watching you and the other business-owning raccoons while I was flying.
When all those other ring-tailed critters fail, they stop trying."
Ralphy reflects:

Are problems opportunities?
Problems teach me exactly what I need when it is needed!
Wisdom comes from problems, heeded!"

Many years pass and Ralphy starts again with all his lessons learned.

Wise Raccoon suddenly appears.
He is impressed that Ralphy never quit, despite the tears.

"Ralphy, you passed every test!
I have brought fellow business raccoons who want to invest."

When the leader and his followers truly work hard, that is worth clapping.
Ralphy now leads employees across the country without the worry of little critters napping.
Without drama, daily success is showing.
Finally, Ralphy's business is really growing.

Years later, Ralphy asks himself: "How was I so lucky to get here?"

Ralphy's Five "Secret" Rules for Success
Rule #1: Never stop trying.
Rule #2: Be careful with whom you associate with. Work with only those who are long-term minded.
Rule #3: Be thrifty.
Rule #4: Take action, especially when things are darkest.
Rule #5: Always remember this: life's problems can be your best friends.

Ralphy is sitting at his desk deep in thought, when a young raccoon barges in and says,

"Yo, Ringo! How do I get rich like you?"